Michael Swanwick's

Field Guide to the
Mesozoic Megafauna

Tachyon Publications
San Francisco

This is a work of fiction. All events portrayed in this book are fictitious, and any resemblance to real people or events is purely coincidental.

Book Design by Eleanor M. Farrell

Cover illustration and interior artwork by Stephanie Pui-Mun Law

Tachyon Publications
1459 18th Street #139
San Francisco, CA 94107
(415) 285-5615

Edited by Jacob Weisman

ISBN: 1-892391-13-9

First Edition: February 2004

Printed in the United States of America by Phoenix Color Corporation

0 9 8 7 6 5 4 3 2 1

Table of Contents

A Field Guide to the Mesozoic Megafauna

Five British Dinosaurs

A Field Guide to Mesozoic Megafauna

The Thief of Time
Eoraptor: early Carnian

There were dinosaurs in the late Triassic, but they were only one group of animals among many, and far from the dominant one. Our expedition was interested in dinosaurs of course, but mostly we were there to study the thecodonts.

There was a wall around our camp to keep out the critters, but life is persistent and every now and then something would get through. I figured that's what had happened when I heard Gregory bellowing in the tent that served as our nursery, and I came running.

For one brief instant I saw an *Eoraptor* posed in front of the nursery tent, clutching something in its forelimbs. *Eoraptor* means "dawn thief." They're small theropods, about three feet long—pygmies compared to the nineteen-foot-long reptilian phytosaurs who were this ecology's dominant carnivores. Still, our guy was going to be a winner. It was ancestral to tyrannosaurs. Phytosaurs were ancestral to nothing.

Then Angela came out and whapped the *Eoraptor* with a camera tripod, and he was gone so fast it seemed like he'd never been there.

Gregory was red with indignation. "Little bastard!" he muttered.

"What was it doing?" I asked.

He glanced back at the nursery, where the incubator in which we'd planned to hatch a clutch of rhynchosaurs lay pried open.

"Stealing our eggs."

A Matter of Size
Giganotosaurus: Albian

Tyrannosaurus rex gets all the fame, all the glory, all the street cred. But the truth is that the largest carnivore ever to walk the earth was *Giganotosaurus*. No kidding, giganotosaurs are bigger. But because giganotosaurs are South American and tyrannosaurs are North American, they just can't get the recognition. The Anglos are more media-savvy. They control all the museums.

Don't think the giganotosaurs aren't aware of this, either. In seedy taverns scattered across the wind-swept pampas of Argentina, giganotosaurs gather in small groups to pop a few beers, down a gaucho or two, and complain about the injustice. "If only," one will inevitably grumble, "there were a connection between the Americas—a land bridge or something—then we'd fix those pipsqueaks! And their little mammals, too!"

Sometimes somebody mentions the existence of Central America, and they all get excited and begin to make plans. But after a few beers, they've forgotten what they were talking about, and return to their griping.

Fortunately for tyrannosaurs, giganotosaurs have extremely tiny brains.

Three Conversations
Quetzalcoatlus: Campanian

"Flying kites again?"

"Sort of."

"What a whopper! It's as big as an airplane. What's it supposed to be—some kind of flying lizard?"

"*Quetzalcoatlus.* The biggest pteranodon there ever was. Thirty-six foot wingspan."

"Uh-oh. Here comes that bully and his dog."

"I'm not afraid."

"Well, I sure am. That's one mean kid. If you need me for anything, I'll be over there by the swings. So I'll have a head start if he comes after me."

" 'kay."

"Hey, *kid*! Didn't I chase you out of here the other day?"

"Yeah."

"So what are you doing back?"

"It's the only good kite-flying spot in town. Open. Up on a hill. The wind's good here."

"Well, I don't like kite-flyers. So beat it."

"It's a free country. I can do what I want."

"You want me to sick Mauler on you again?"

"Just try it."

"All right, you asked for it. Mauler! Sic 'im, boy! Sic 'im! Sic … oh, my God."

"Serves you right."

"You … that … that thing ate my dog!"

"He was hungry."

"It didn't have the right to do that!"

"Well, you didn't have the right to sic your dog on me."

"Hey! Tell your thing to stop staring at me."

"He's probably still hungry. If I were you, I'd get out of here. Fast."

"You don't think it would …?"

"*Run!*"

"Wow. That bully really tore out of here. I don't think he likes your—what did you call it?"

"*Quetzalcoatlus*. My dad whipped him up in the lab."

"I thought it was just a kite."

"That's why I tied a string to one foot."

"Huh? Why?"

"So people would underestimate him."

How the West Was Won II
Triceratops: late Maastrichtian

Triceratops is the other *other* white meat. When, in a miracle of modern genetic engineering, it was resurrected from the dustbin of history, it quickly became the fad herd animal of agricultural entrepreneurs. Ten years after their reintroduction, triceratops outnumbered buffalo on the Great Plains.

Just as the Plains Indians had taken to that European introduction, the horse, as if they had been its masters from the dawn of time, so too they took to the triceratops. It became a part of their customs, their rituals, their lives.

Down in Texas, whole-body triceratops barbeques were predictably popular. Planeloads of Japanese tourists flew in for a traditional hoedown and dino-roast. They were all anxious to see an Apache triceratops-dance.

Within a generation, Western history had been completely re-mythologized. Wagon trains had been drawn by mamenchisaurs. Cochise rode a tyrannosaur. The U.S. Cavalry mounted fleet gallimimuses. It was all nonsense, of course. But it was profitable nonsense. So that was the past everyone agreed upon.

Historians grumbled, of course. But even they had to admit that the new myth of the West was no worse than the previous set of lies everybody had believed in.

The Scientific Method
Pachycephalosaurus: late Maastrichtian

Pachycephalosaurus was the largest and most advanced of all bone-headed dinos. The top of its skull was a dome of thick bone. "You could whack away at it all day with a hammer and never leave a mark," Ralph Chapman said happily. Ralph was a big fan of pachycephalosaurs. That was why he had been chosen for this expedition. "Looks like we've got a little intraspecific combat going on here, too."

Two pachycephalosaurs butted heads in the distance. They looked a lot like mountain goats, only larger and more dinosaurian.

Dr. Bailey snorted. "So, yes, fine, you're right. Those domed skulls are used by the males to establish dominance within the herd. That doesn't mean I'm not *also* right. Those skulls could be used aggressively against other species as well."

Ralph clasped his hands behind his back. "We haven't seen it happen yet," he said mildly.

"Lack of evidence is not the same thing as proof!"

"Then come up with some proof."

"All right, I will!" Dr. Bailey snatched up the inflato-velociraptor and charged straight at the nearest pachycephalosaur. The inflato-velociraptor was an air-filled device intended for use in recording the reactions of other species to the presence of a velociraptor. It was not meant to be used as a shield. But Dr. Bailey was headstrong. He pushed the rubber device ahead of himself as if it would provide him with the least scintilla of protection. Which it patently did not.

The pachycephalosaur saw what it thought was a predator coming straight at it. It lowered its head and charged.

The inflato-velociraptor went bouncing into the air like the balloon that it was. The pachycephalosaur's skull crashed into Dr. Bailey's. He fell down, dead.

“Well, damn,” Ralph said. “You learn something new every day.”

He wasn’t really upset at being proved wrong, though. He was a scientist. And the great thing about science was that all facts were provisional. If it turned out your pet theory was wrong, you simply shrugged and moved on.

Dueling Mosasaurs
Mosasaurus: Turonian

We ran the mosasaurs off radio-controlled biochips with a joystick interface. Thumb controls for direction and speed, shoulder buttons for "comatose," "feeding frenzy," and other essential functions. Mostly we used them to herd the Turonian ocean life so our paleomarine biologists could study and sample them. But on our off-time, Chuck and I fought duels.

Mosasaurs are terrifying creatures. Forty-foot-long marine reptiles with tooth-filled mouths like a knife-grinder's nightmare. Which made it particularly unfortunate that nobody told us that the President of Western Mars would be scuba diving right smack-dab in the center of our dueling grounds.

How our duels worked was we swam our mosasaurs apart, so they could build up some speed, then drove them straight at each other. It was your basic game of chicken, with the proviso that if your critter got bitten or scraped you automatically lost. So we brought 'em together with their jaws snapping, to encourage the other to veer away first.

Poor President Richards! Imagine seeing one of these monsters coming straight at you and turning to flee, only to be confronted by its twin.

He screamed. I know so because Chuck caught it on his mosa-cam just before yanking his beast aside so it wouldn't endanger the man.

We were still laughing when President Richards's bodyguards came in and had a few words with us.

The press conference is in ten minutes. Both Chuck and I are terribly sorry we accidentally endangered this great man. We were astonished by how calmly he faced death. His jaw got firm. He didn't close his eyes. It's a pity our cameras weren't on to record this heroic moment.

That's our story anyway, and we're sticking to it.

Pocket Brontosaurs
Apatosaurus: Kimmeridgian-Tithonian

The ethics of genetic engineering get tangled fast. Nobody denied that cloning dinosaurs from fossil DNA was a good thing. Only a few objected to using gene therapy to optimize their health. But creating a six-inch-long apatosaur was just plain *wrong*.

"We're going to call them brontosaurs," the marketing director said. "It's sexier. Every kid in the world will want one."

"I refuse to go along with this," I said.

"Scientists re-named the buggers based on which fossils were identified first," the lawyer said. "It doesn't have the force of law. We can use any trade name we wish."

"No, I mean these animals shouldn't be created in the first place. An *Apatosaurus* was an enormous animal. Making it tiny is like creating a legless horse or a flightless eagle. It's a violation of the natural order, dammit."

"You're just the bioethicist," said the project chief. "Who gave you the authority to stop this? You're not God!"

"More to the point, we've got millions tied up in this project already," the accountant said. "There's no way the brass would let you stand in the way."

"Then I'll quit!"

Nobody said anything.

On the way out of the building, I stopped by security to drop off my ID badge for the last time. The guard on duty was a heavy-set woman named Jessamine. She knew I was with the project. "Tell me something." She leaned forward confidentially. "These teeny little dinosaurs—they really gonna be the hot toy this Christmas?" She had an eight-year-old. It was information she needed to know.

"Oh yeah," I said sadly. "Trust me on this one. They're going to be bigger than big."

Herbivores
Iguanodon: Valanginian-Barremian

I was hitchhiking outside of Oklahoma City when I caught a ride with a migrating iguanodon in a Chevy Suburban.

"Being a herbivore is a real bitch," he said, taking a last drag on his Winston and flicking the butt out the window. "You're always on the move. Looking for forage, keeping an eye out for predators. No wonder I got ulcers."

"Those predators are a problem, huh?"

"Don't get me started! I had a run-in with a pack of allosaurs outside of Lubbock last week. Lost two buddies and my Uncle Dave. Third attack in a year! My insurance premiums are out of sight! That's with a deductible like nobody's business. But what can you do? You watch what you eat, you always use your safety belt, and odds are some snotty little theropod's gonna get you anyway."

"Theropods are a problem, then."

"They're the worst! Sneaky little bastards. They've got a million tricks. You think you're safe and—wham! they've got you! Just when you least expect it." He pounded the steering wheel with annoyance. "But enough about me. What's your story, Mac? You look to be some kind of *Tenontosaurus*, right?"

"Right," I said. "Hey, would you mind pulling over for a moment? There's something I gotta do."

"Call of nature, eh?" He chuckled. "Sure, why not?"

As the iguanodon slowed the SUV, I surreptitiously put a hand to the zipper of my disguise. Only a couple more seconds, and I had him.

Herbivores! You gotta love 'em. They fall for the old theropod-in-a-rubber-tenontosaur-suit trick every time.

Parallels

Troodon: late Campanian–early Maastrichtian

The parallels are striking. A typical adult troodon was about six feet long. A typical adult human is about six feet tall. A troodon's eyes were set on the front of its face, as in humans, not on the sides, as in most other dinos. Troodons were bipedal. So are we.

Troodon was the smartest of all dinosaurs.

Homo sapiens is the smartest of all mammals.

Troodons lived in an age of massive worldwide extinctions. So do humans—in fact, the extinctions appear to have begun simultaneous with our own rise as a species. They've accelerated since the beginning of the industrial revolution, of course. But they've been going on for a long time.

Troodon died off abruptly in the Maastrichtian age.

Analogies can be pushed too far.

Wusses
Hadrosaurus: Campanian

Our time machine shifted silently into being in the middle of a Mesozoic swamp. Bob Walters and I stepped out onto a small, sandy island. Bob had been there-and-then before. This was my first time. Bob nudged me and pointed upward.

"Holy cow," I whispered, "look at the size of that monster!"

It was a *Hadrosaurus*—your quintessentially average-sized duckbill dinosaur.

Average size in this case being twenty-five-feet long. It had reared up on its hind legs to get at the tender foliage of a metasequoia tree. It was perfectly oblivious to us, despite the fact that we were literally standing in its shadow.

"Let's get the heck out of here," I suggested.

"Phaw!" Bob whispered back. "These guys are harmless. They're the biggest wusses in the Mesozoic. Watch this. I bet I can make it faint."

He waved his arms and shouted, "*Boo!*"

Just as predicted, the hadrosaur fainted.

Right on top of our time machine.

Dinosaur Music
Parasaurolophus: late Campanian–Maastrichtian

Parasaurolophus is distinguished by a curved bone crest, twice as long as the rest of its skull. Two hollow tubes run to the tip of the crest and back again. When air is forced through them, it makes an extraordinary sound—deep, lingering, resonant, and haunting.

Time travelers from the Telezoic, a hundred million years beyond the era of the human race, come to the Cretaceous to tame and train parasaurolophs so they can put on concerts. These events, which can last for weeks, attract representatives from a dozen intelligent races, scattered across four billion years of time.

These concerts are a hot-ticket item, to be sure. But everyone agrees that the absolute best musical events ever are those rare occasions when parasaurolophs are brought forward to the Cenozoic, for duets with the humpbacked whales.

The Bird-Fishers
Elasmosaurus

Chinese fisher-folk are extremely conservative. They have used cormorants to catch fish for at least a thousand years. They place rings around the birds' necks so they can't swallow, and train them to bring their catch to the fishing-boats.

So when scientists in Beijing resurrected *Elasmosaurus*, the largest and longest marine reptile ever, it only made sense that the pragmatic fisher-folk would place rings around their long, long necks, and train them to hunt sea birds.

Japanese salesmen say, "We can build you robot lizards that will catch birds far more efficiently." But the Chinese are not convinced. They say, "Can you build a robot that runs on meat scraps and fish entrails? Will it breed its own replacement before it wears out?"

The fisher-folk's children like to grab onto an elasmosaur's neck-ring and catch a ride, soaring underwater for ten and twenty minutes at a time. They can do this, of course, because they all have gills.

When you make your living from the sea, in constant danger of drowning, gills are a good thing to have. So they're retro-engineered into the children at birth. Because Chinese fisher-folk are extremely conservative.

Proving Dr. Tom's Hypothesis
Tyrannosaurus: late Maastrichtian

Sam and I aren't paleontologists. We're physicists. To us, the time machine was just a good hardware hack. We didn't have any specific plans for it. But when Dr. Tom heard we'd built it, he started jumping up and down, and burbling about tyrannosaurid ancestry (it's that boyish enthusiasm that makes everybody attach the honorific to his first name, rather than his last), and, well, that's how we all ended up in the Cretaceous.

"Now, let me get this straight," I said. "You want to prove that birds are descended from *tyrannosaurs*?"

"No, no, birds are descended from maniraptors. But maniraptors are a sister clade to tyrannosaurs, and they're both nested within the coleurosaurian theropods. Distant cousins, sort of. Now, if I've got this right, tyrannosaurs should display several bird-like characteristics that haven't been preserved in the fossil record."

"Such as?"

"Well, feathers, for—"

At that instant a *Tyrannosaurus rex* burst out of the jungle. It was enormous, and would have been terrifying if it hadn't been covered with bright yellow feathers. It looked like the world's biggest budgerigar.

It swung that massive head around, fixing its malevolent gaze on Dr. Tom. Then it opened its mouth and roared, "CHIRP!"

We were still laughing when the tyrannosaur ate Dr. Tom.

Five British Dinosaurs

Iguanodon anglicus

It was Mary Ann Mantell who discovered the first *Iguanodon* fossils, in the South Downs of Sussex. She was a doctor's wife and had accompanied her husband on his rounds, when she was attacked by pixies.

It was a lovely day and, since Mary shared her husband's interests in natural history and geology in particular, she stayed outside while Gideon went into a patient's house.

He'd only been gone a few minutes when two or more invisible, giggling imps began pelting stones at Mary. Small, hard pebbles struck her on the arms and shoulders. Though she could see perfectly well from whence these missiles came, there appeared to be no one there. That, and the small, wicked voices, told her what her tormentors were.

A doctor's wife in Sussex of the 1820s was no weak and simpering thing. Without hesitation, she ran to a nearby pile of gravel (the road was being graded) and proceeded to give as good as she got. Then she spotted something white in the gravel. It was a tooth, embedded in rock.

When Gideon Algernon Mantell emerged into the sunlight again, Mary had gone through the entire pile of gravel, and had a handful of teeth to show him. The pixies, capricious as ever, had stopped their barrage when she had, and were now gone about their mysterious ways.

Dr. Mantell published a description of the teeth as belonging to a gigantic Mesozoic lizard which he named *Iguanodon*, or "lizard-tooth" in 1825. It was a fine piece of research, and only the second dinosaur (though the term "dinosaur" did not yet exist) ever described.

Mary never told anyone of the part the Little People had played in her discovery. A new era of scientific discovery was dawning across Europe, and fairies were no longer entirely respectable.

Yaverlandia bitholus

Prior to our discovery, *Yaverlandia* was known only from a single fragmentary skull excavated from the Wealdon Marls in the Isle of Wight. Imagine our astonishment when our expedition (Chapman, Brett-Surman et al.) discovered a living specimen of this least-known of all pachycephalosaurs holding down a rather exalted civil service position in Whitehall!

With some difficulty, we obtained an interview.

"Oh, the usual," he said when Dr. Brett-Surman asked him how he made his living. "I keep my head down, I try to keep the other chaps off my turf."

"And head-butting?" Ralph Chapman asked.

"Well, I *am* a bureaucrat, after all."

"How do you like the modern world? I asked.

"Things were infinitely better run in the Mesozoic," the *Yaverlandia* said firmly. "One associated with a better class of being. Admittedly, theropods were a bit of a problem. But mammals knew their place then."

"Are there more of your species about? Surely your existence argues that there must be a breeding population somewhere."

"I am a widower. My wife died, along with all the rest of my kind, at the end of the Cretaceous, sixty-five million years ago."

"But how on Earth," I cried, "have you managed to survive all the millions of years that separate the Mesozoic from the modern day?"

"I'm afraid I'm not cleared to give you that information," the *Yaverlandia* replied stiffly. And showed us the door.

Altispinax dunkeri

Like so many of Ray Harryhausen's films, the plot was unworthy of him. But when your talent is for special effects and your special genius lies in the creation of dinosaurs, you take what work you can get. Still, even for Hammer Studios, *Bertie Wooster and the Dinosaurs* was a particularly ripe notion.

Somehow, though, the movie was put into production.

Ordinarily, Harryhausen favored stop-motion animation. It chanced, however, that a friend in the Ministry of Defense knew of two experimental bipedal walking-machines that were being scrapped and could be picked up for a song. They were shaped and sized just right for a pair of *Altispinax*—fleet, sail-backed theropods.

He re-geared the cams to lengthen the stride, then fitted both with small, powerful gasoline engines. Lastly, he sheathed them in molded latex, so that they looked the part of living and carnivorous dinosaurs. There was a cockpit midway down the back of each. In operation, the driver would be hidden by the sail. But for the shakedown run, he left the sails undeployed.

It was nighttime when he was finally done. Harryhausen turned to his assistant and, with a courtly little bow, said, "Well, young lady—care to take 'em out for a spin?"

Tess leapt into a cockpit. "Yes, *sir*!"

A minute later, the two *Altispinax* sped into the night.

It was a wild run. Cars braked wildly and slid into ditches at the sight of the two prehistoric monsters running side-by-side down Maidenstone Road. Dogs barked savagely after them. Children stared wide-eyed from bedroom windows.

The stride was smooth—Harryhausen had put a great deal of thought into the shocks—and quiet, too. Twice they ran past patrol cars, the faces of the officers within stiff and white with disbelief. They ran all the way from the studio at Bray to the steps of the British Museum. Laughing, Harryhausen drew up his beast, and made it dance in place, lifting up those great legs and setting them down with exquisite delicacy. Tess threw back her theropod's throat and, putting hands to mouth, let out a howl that would shiver spines if they decided to use it in the movie.

A paleontologist, letting himself out by a side door after a late evening's work, glanced up at the two dinosaurs and sniffed. "You're not fooling anyone, you know," he said. He pointed to the feet. "The toes are all wrong, and the hallux is reversed."

And, so saying, he went home.

Megalosaurus bucklandii

Megalosaurus was the first dinosaur ever named, and one of three (the others were *Iguanodon* and *Hylaeosaurus*, both discovered by the energetic Gideon Mantell) that caused Richard Owen to create the grouping *Dinosauria*. Alas, the species remains something of a dust-bin for large, difficult-to-attribute theropods. The original specimen, found in a quarry at Stonesfield in Oxfordshire and described by William Buckland, was fragmentary in the extreme. Which helps to explain the sculptor Benjamin Waterhouse Hawkins's reconstructions.

Waterhouse Hawkins was commissioned by Owen to create life-sized statues of his newly-named dinosaurs for the grounds of the Crystal Palace. The results—heavy, lumbering, and evil of visage—were an enormous success. A dinner party held within the body of the *Iguanodon*, just before its completion, was one of the great scientific social events of the Victorian era.

It was not long afterwards that a *Megalosaurus* called upon Waterhouse Hawkins in person.

It looked nothing like he had imagined. It was a biped, for one thing, and properly attired for another. Stooping its head, so it could pass through his doorway, it entered his flat with hat and gloves in one hand, and presented him with its card. Its manners were impeccable. He had no choice but to invite it in for tea.

"My dear fellow," the *Megalosaurus* began. "You cannot possibly imagine the distress you have caused me by your uncouth representations." It shuddered. "You have me crawling about the ground on all fours, like a common beast! The expression upon my face is that of one who is a slave to his baser emotions." It took a delicate sip from its cup. Waterhouse Hawkins could not but note how delicately it held out its third finger. "And yet, as you can see, I am quite a civilized creature."

"The difficulties presented by incomplete fossils—" Waterhouse Hawkins began.

"Yes, yes, of course. One understands, and one sympathizes. Yet consider my position. Consider my reputation! I must ask for a retraction."

"I worked, sir, with the leading comparative anatomists of Europe. Had you presented yourself while we were consulting on the designs, we should certainly have taken your self-characterization into account. However, you did not."

"But—"

"At any rate, the models were extraordinarily expensive to fabricate. There is no money left to have them redone."

The *Megalosaurus* stood. "You leave me with no choice but to consult a solicitor."

Waterhouse Hawkins stood as well. Coldly, he said, "I content myself with the knowledge that there is not a lawyer in London who would accept as a client a gigantic carnivorous reptile."

With an angry clash of teeth, the *Megalosaurus* seized his hat and left.

Waterhouse Hawkins would have taken it all for a dream, save for the fact that he saw the dinosaur once again. It was a Sunday, and he was out for a stroll when he spied the *Megalosaurus* coming toward him on the sidewalk. It was the exact same creature—there was no possible way of mistaking it for anyone else.

Nor could he avoid it. Common courtesy required that he smile and nod as it passed. So he did.

The brute looked at him … and then *through* him. It cut him! Waterhouse Hawkins stood trembling and outraged. He had been snubbed, by God. The monstrous beast had cut him dead!

Craterosaurus pottonensis

Our coven hired a small bus to take us to Bedfordshire, where we intended to raise the spirit of a *Craterosaurus*—bones of one such stegosaurid had been found there, so it seemed a good bet. We had a pleasant drive, and sang old camp songs, rather to the dismay of our driver, and then retired to our rooms to get some sleep, so we'd be fresh for the event. Midnight found us in an appropriately spooky cemetery (mood, after all, matters) with the twelve of us, male and female alike, sky-clad, and our necromancer in Druidic robes.

We had brought a rather nice trilobite fossil to sacrifice. After the appropriate ceremonies Tim, the necromancer, smashed it to powder with one blow of a hammer, and shouted the Word of Summoning.

Out from the ground rose bone after bone, assembling themselves into the complete skeleton of a *Craterosaurus*. Earth flowed over the bones, became muscle, and sprouted skin. The great brute shook its head and opened its eyes. It studied us a moment in silence. Then—

"You're naked," it said.

Jane Giddings blushed. (There are those who'd say that seeing Jane naked was in and of itself reason enough to join the coven, and I'd not be one to gainsay them.) "We're not ashamed of our bodies," she told the ghostly animal. And stood so straight I could hardly catch my breath.

"Oh," it said, in a tone that indicated it was beginning to find us all rather boring. "Well, I suppose you've got some questions for me. Out with them."

There was a moment's silence. I don't think any of us had prepared questions. We'd decided to raise the *Craterosaurus* more for the challenge of the thing than with any particular end in view. On an impulse, I said, "How did the dinosaurs die out?"

"Haven't the foggiest. After my time. When I was alive, everything was going swimmingly." It yawned. "Next question."

But neither, it turned out, did the *Craterosaurus* know anything about climatic shifts or ecological issues. Nor did it know if it was warm-blooded or cold-blooded ("Define your terms," it said, and it turned out that none of us *could*), or whether birds were really and truly descended from dinosaurs, or who was going to win this year's World Cup. That last question was Tim's. A good necromancer, was Tim, but not the brightest bulb on the porch.

Finally, we all got as tired of the conversation as the spirit of the *Craterosaurus* was, and sent it back to its eternal rest. "What a stupid beast!" Ian muttered to me, as we were all getting dressed afterwards. "As far as I'm concerned, this has been a complete and utter waste of time."

"Oh, I don't know." I glanced over at Jane Giddings, who was busily buttoning up her blouse. As soon as she was fully dressed, I was going to march right over to her and ask her out. "I personally learned rather a lot tonight."